Clint Faraday
book forty one
Live the Easy Way
Die the Hard Way

Clint is in Pedasi, visiting friends. There is a man there who is known for various scams that rob people of their property and money. He is in a casino with three local girls and is winning at blackjack

Mario says he sure is living it up the easy way. Maybe sometimes crime does pay!

Clint replies that living the easy way, in that one's case, can lead to dying the hard way.

The scam artist dies – the hard way. The *really* hard way!

This book is based on a character I have met.

Contents

About the Author

CD Moulton has traveled extensively over much of the world both in the music business, where he was a rock guitarist, songwriter, and arranger, and in an import/export business. He has been everything from a bar owner to auto salvage (junkyard) manager, longshoreman to high steel worker, orchid grower to landscaper, tropical fish farmer to commercial fisherman. He started writing books in 1983 and has published more than 200 books as of January 1, 2013. His most popular books to date are about research with orchids, though much of his science fiction and fantasy work has proven popular. He wrote the CD Grimes, PI series and the Det. Nick Storie series, among other works.

He now resides in David, Panamá, where he writes the Clint Faraday mystery series, plays music with friends – and pursues his favorite ways to spend his time: beach bum and roaming the mountains doing botanical research. He has recently become involved in fighting the corruption that is rampant in the legal and judicial system. "I love Panama' and that is hurting this country badly."

CD is involved in research of natural cancer cure at this time. It has proven effective in all cases, so far. It is based on a plant that has been in use for thousands of years, is safe, available, and cheap. He has studied botany, and was cured of a serious lymphoma with use of the plant, *Ambrosia peruviana*.

Information about this cure is free on the FaceBook page, Ambrosia peruviana for cancer. CD asks only that all who try it please report on its effectiveness on that group.

Live the Easy Way
Die the Hard Way

<u>*Pedasi*</u>

Clint watched the country going by outside the window. It was a slightly cloudy day, but bright. He was riding the bus, this trip, not driving. He was able to talk with people and enjoy just being in this paradise.

There weren't so many of the people he most related to on this trip. There were eight or ten tourists and quite a few business people going to Las Tablas from Santiago. The bus was crowded to the point all the seats were taken. The driver had the music too loud, but that was almost a routine thing, on these trips. The Panamanians like a lot of noise. It's cultural.

He was making a vacation of this trip. He had a job, in a way. He was trying to locate a man and woman who had embezzled a large sum from one of his personal projects

Clint, Judi Lum, his smart attractive Oriental next door neighbor in Bocas Town, and Manny Matthews had spent several millions of dollars on various projects to help the Indigenos. They were building two clinics and a large school, right now. The people, Harry Arnolds and his Panamanian wife, Gloria Arrends, had absconded with more than two million dollars from the clinic building fund. They were lately reported to have been seen several times around the Pedasi area and around Playa Venado and up to Pocri. He would quietly find them and explain some of the facts of life to them.

He was seated with a bunch of tourists from Canada and England. He'd rather be with the Indios, but them were the breaks. Carol Fine, Ontario, said that the scenery before had gotten a little dull, but it was certainly getting better, now that they were approaching the Pacific coast. Benny Goode, London, agreed about the scenery being better, but said he hadn't seen anywhere in Panamá that he would call dull. Even the cattle country around Santiago was different enough to be interesting.

Carol and Benny were in the seats to his left.

Pete Milton, Liverpool, seated next to him by the window, agreed that Panamá was a very scenic place everywhere he'd been.

Sandra Vincente, Quebec, seated just in back to the left, said she had really liked the islands in the Caribbean and she would certainly like the Las Tablas area. She heard the Pacific beaches were beautiful. She was seated next to a quiet older man from Charlotte, W. Va. He hadn't spoken much at all during the whole trip. He seemed lost in thought, much of the time. He spent a lot of time on a laptop.

He spoke now. "The Pacific is beautiful, and I agree that the whole country is. I particularly like the mountainous river types of places, myself. I bought a large place near Gualaca. Five hundred hectares, with a little river running through it and another smaller one as one property line.

"The Pacific is dangerous, so be careful. The extreme tides cause undertows that can carry you out to sea before you can react. Don't fight them, swim along with them and angle back in. Sharks *in the water* aren't a great problem, here.

"The mountains can be as dangerous, in other ways. The sharks *there* are a problem.

"Don't trust anyone with anything important. That's something you have to be very careful of, here. There are people who are more dangerous than any tide or place.

"Sorry. Personal. Just be very careful."

His laptop dinged. He excused himself and said he'd just downloaded a free e-book that almost described his situation.

"It's a thing called *Fading Paradise*. It's being updated, regularly. A man who has had his entire retirement stolen and has been fighting a corrupt legal system for three years, trying to get some kind of justice."

"A friend writes it," Clint said. "He's been going through hell with it. He doesn't let it get to him. He says he loves Panamá and the people and has friends. He tries to spend most of his time with the Indios and live in their culture – as do I. My wife and two children are in a place called Cusapín, on the Caribbean. It's paradise.

"I think President Martinelli is cleaning up a good bit of the corruption in Panamá City. I also thinks he as much as ignores it in Chiriqui and Bocas.

"Let's not get into politics. I try to stay out of it, and so does he."

They changed the subject to other, more pleasant topics. Jenny Roberts, Ontario, said she and Carol had been to Cusapín. It was paradise, but there was nothing to do there. She liked places with night life.

Clint told them he was headed for Pedasi, which wasn't nearly so developed as Las Tablas.

They stopped in Chitre, a large city. They were there two hours, then went on another bus. They pulled into Las Tablas and separated. Clint would stay the night and go to Pedasi in the morning. Charles said he was going to Pedasi, himself. He had to meet someone there.

In the morning, Clint had a good breakfast and went to

the bus for Pedasi. Charles was there with three other gringos he introduced as Lucas "Luke" Ford and Sam Crane from Austin, Texas, and Larry Simms from Macon, Georgia. Benny Goode also came to the bus. He said he'd asked about the place because Clint had mentioned it. He'd decided to see it, while he was this close. Las Tablas was a lot of fun and a little different, but it was like a lot of other places.

"Oh? You aren't traveling as a group?" Charles asked.

"No. I think the others are together, but I met them in Santiago. They were coming here, I was coming here."

There were about fifteen others for the bus. Seven were Indios, so Clint managed to join them and sat closer to the back of the bus. The others sat as near the front as they could. Larry Simms sat about the middle and was talking with a big black man who was in the military in the states during Vietnam. Larry was saying he had some pretty mean experiences, but after Vietnam. Afghanistan. Iran. He had been in special forces. Typical BS among vets.

They got into Pedasi close to ten o'clock and found lodging. Clint was offered a place at Mario Valencia's house. He accepted (he was declared Ngobe by the council, the second white man ever, and was damned proud of it!). He was a different tribe, but these were very like his people. Mario introduced Clint to his lady, Jessy (pronounced Yessy) Ra. She was a very pretty India. Mario said he thought she was pregnant. He would marry her, if she was.

They spent the day with Mario showing Clint around the area. It was only the second time Clint had been there. They ran into others Clint had met, and came across Charles and company, as Clint labeled them, now and again.

After a delicious dinner, Mario took Clint to the local brothel. Clint said he was married and that was that, but he wanted to see the place. It had a small casino as part of it.

A man was there with three local girls hanging on him. He wasn't so attractive, that Clint could see, so he had money. He seemed to really be living it up.

"What? He hit the lottery?" Clint asked.

"That's Koko Perez. He's a ladron. He sounds really good, but he's a thief! He steals everything from old people. He takes everything they have!

"I don't understand it. He steals ten thousand dollars today and has a couple of hundred dollars tonight and is limpia tomorrow!

"He does live the easy way. Maybe crime does pay!"

"The type lives the easy way and dies the hard way," Filo Mendez, an Indio friend they were with, prophesied. "He will steal something from someone who is not going to allow it.

"He steals for others. He will steal a hundred thousand dollars and they give him a thousand and he thinks he's a bigshot. He has a brain the size of a lentil! If they think he will expose them, they will kill him, and never again think of him for one second. The life is not often worth the death."

Clint had heard of Koko Perez, scam artist, in David. Nothing good.

"He thinks he buys respect. You cannot buy respect. He is pathetic.

"Talk to him, Clint. He will sound so good and like he is your best friend ever in the world! He will have a deal where you can make triple your money in ten days, guaranteed! He knows the people who are planning this bigtime project and there is little time left to get into it, but he has spent everything he has because it cannot lose!

"You give him the money. He takes it to these people in Santiago or David or Panamá City. He will come back with your profit in two days!

"You never see him again. He waits until you are gone, then finds another he can steal from."

"If you do find him somewhere, he is crying because they took all his money and yours. If you listen to that, he will have a way to get it all back. All he needs is a *little* financing and it's done!" Mario said. "I think that he will not scam Clint. Maybe Clint will scam him?"

"Clint will simply not have anything to do with him," Clint said.

They had a beer and sat at a table to talk with some of the locals. Charles and Luke came in and were heading for the bar when Koko laughed louder than he had been. Charles looked at him and stiffened. He said something to Luke and the two turned around and walked out. Koko didn't see them.

Clint remembered Charles had said something about just such a situation. He had downloaded *Fading Paradise* and had said it was a lot like his situation.

Clint didn't think much more about it. He hadn't been asked to do anything. Maybe Charles had an issue with Koko. Maybe he would resolve it in his own way. If the situation were like in the book, he would be trying to get something from the courts or police.

That wasn't likely, if you like understatement.

Clint went to Distilladeros the next day to visit some friends. It was a very tranquil spot and the fishing was good. He lazed around and visited. He casually asked if anyone had seen Harry and Gloria, who were supposed to be living around there since they left Bocas.

They had a place on Playa Venado. Out in the middle of nowhere. It was a very pretty place, but there was nothing to do there. It was too isolated. Gloria liked to shop and go to nice restaurants and shows, Harry liked to lay around and do nothing but fish. He liked golf, which he gave up to be there, and Gloria liked society things, which she gave up to be there. A big crash was coming in their lives. There seemed to be some kind of problem about true ownership of the land, which wasn't really a problem, because the gringos who weren't even in Panamá anymore hadn't really ever owned the place, so couldn't have sold it to Harry. Those Velasquez people were nothing but cheap hoods and ladrones. Harry wasn't the only one they had done that to.

He asked about the Velasquez people.

"They are big shot corrupt politicians in Chitre. They sell land they don't own and cars they don't own and boats they don't own. The court won't even listen to the many denunciados filed against them. They pay the police and the judges to not investigate."

"Koko involved?"

"Far too many of the times. He gets Harry to buy that place for half a million that Velasquez doesn't own, then he gets maybe five hundred dollars for doing it. He's so stupid!"

Clint agreed with that. He went back to Pedasi for the night. It seemed things were fairly tranquil, there. He ran into Benny Goode, who had found a female interest and decided to stay a week, at least. Clint met Toria and noted she had been with Koko in the casino the other night. When she left, he warned Benny that he had to be very careful with women he met in a bar.

"I know exactly what she is. I know what she's doing," he answered. "I saw her with a guy everyone says is a con artist. She's the type I like. To fuck, nothing else. I acted like I have a lot of money and I might want to invest in something in this area.

"I get just enough to get by. I couldn't invest in a lottery ticket. I saw her run right to him when I asked that Gordo character if he knew of a place close where I could get some land cheap. Land on the water.

"She suddenly found me irresistible! I'm so-o-o sexy!"

"Be careful when he learns that you can't buy anything."

"I already have them thinking I have to go to Chitre Monday to transfer funds because I'm flat until I can get a few thousand sent over. I'll keep going from there and won't look back."

"*If* you can convince them that's what you're doing. *They*'re cons!"

"Why, I'll leave clothes and stuff in the hotel room and pay for the night. It's already paid, as a matter of fact. I got the deal where you pay for six nights and get the seventh free. I got a bunch of old clothes from a shop and an old maleta. I picked up some shaving stuff and tooth-paste in the dollar store. It'll be right there, waiting, when I get back.

"When I came here, it was to be for two nights and I didn't bring anything. It's in a locker box in Chitre. If I leave everything here, I'm obviously going to come back! Isn't that obvious?"

"Con the cons. Good luck!"

He grinned and went on. Clint caught a bus to Playa Venado and got off not far from where the house was described as being. It was a nice place. It was a beach chateau type of building, all tile and fancy concrete work with a terra cotta roof over steel cabriola. The view across the Pacific was spectacular. There was a new Mercedes in the carport.

Clint went up the red brick path to ring the doorbell. There was a pause, then Gloria, dressed in a skirt and apron, answered. She saw Clint and almost fainted. She squealed and tried to slam the door. Clint shoved it and said, "How uncooth! I come all the way out here to visit and you treat me this way!

"We have to have a little talk."

"Harry!" she screeched. He came running in and almost fell over when he saw Clint there.

"Just wanted to explain that you have ten days to have two million dollars back into the account. I won't pursue it further, unless you fail to get the money deposited.

"Really nice place. The location is perfect, for one thing, the view, but stinks, for other reasons, to most people. Sorta isolated. You could die of a heart attack out here and no one would know for months."

"We don't have close to that much money!" Gloria cried.

"You stole that much money. I don't give a damn where you get it, but you pay that money back into the fund or you face the law."

Harry almost smirked. "I guess we won't have any choice but to face the law, then."

"Comarca law. It was them you stole from."

"Er! We, uh, we can raise maybe one million, but we can't ... I mean! This place! It's worth a million! How about, we give you a million and this place?"

"Except the point this isn't your place. It belongs to the Lanchesters, back in the states, but even that's in question. It's worth maybe half a million."

"Dear god! We have no way to raise another million dollars!" Gloria squealed.

"Oh! One other thing!" Clint said. "To try this stunt on anyone wasn't exactly smart. To pull it on a detective who spends his life finding people for various reasons is just plain stupid beyond belief! There's noplace you can run to.

"I'll get back to Pedasi. I don't want to waste a lot of time on this. You might make a deal with Manny and Judi for the million plus whatever else on time payments, or something. Me, I'd just handle ... well! See you around!"

He walked out with them standing there, staring.

Back in Pedasi, he saw Charles and Luke. They had a very good dinner in a little restaurant Clint knew. It was local seafood that was prepared just right. They talked about various odd things. Sam Crane came in soon to join them.

Finally, Luke said, "Clint, are you the detective I've heard a lot about lately?"

"I'm a detective."

"Can I give you a retainer and have guaranteed confidentiality?"

"You have that, no matter what, unless you're into something illegal or unethical."

"I've heard that. Would a hundred dollars make it official?"

"No. This isn't the states. Only the church can guarantee

that things will stay there. Even in the states, only religion and doctors have any legally guaranteed confidentiality.

"It about Koko and Velasquez?"

They all looked shocked. "How did..!?" Charles cried.

"I'm a detective. They're known hoods. You made the remarks about a situation like in *Fading Paradise*. A friend writes that. Any such situation that would bring you here is around those cruds. Two and two is still four."

"What can we do?" Luke asked.

"Tell me about it. Condensed. I know the basic con."

Charles cleared his throat. "I didn't know Luke or Sam until we met, back in Santiago. There is a detective Luke brought here from Texas. He says Perez can't be touched with this corrupt legal system here and Velasquez probably can't. If we file charges through the courts, we'll wait three or four years for them to say they can't find the evidence to take to court and a crooked judge will halt the investigation. Just like the book."

"Did they pull the scam with a crooked notary and contracts in Spanish that you didn't understand?" Clint asked.

"With me and Sam. Luke had what he thought was a clear title. It's just suddenly registered in another name."

"A contract written in Spanish with a person who doesn't speak or read Spanish has to be presented with a copy translation into whatever language or a statement on the contract that it was translated by such and such a person," Clint lectured. "That contract is fraud. By law."

"Which means absolutely nothing, when they refuse to act on that law," Luke said. "They get paid not to act.

"Where do we go from here?"

"With the law, until there are changes, you're stuck filing new charges every year. You can contest if they try to sell the land and keep them tied up in court for years, but that's about all. You may be able to find someone who can scam the scammers. It's a matter of having the money to finance that."

"So. We find our own Koko to scam Velasquez back out of our land. That means a lot of money we don't have, anymore, so the system goes on and on," Sam said.

"A Koko doesn't cost much. Make a deal like they make with him. He's going to get rich when they have the land. When they get it into their name, they have to sell it before they can pay him anything, but here's a couple hundred to tide him over until they do sell it.

"When they do sell it, he gets another hundred bucks. He's a pathetic idiot! He's just a goat and could be getting the land in his own name the same way and not take anymore risk than he is now. No matter what, he gets the blame, if there's any to get."

"You're supposed to be pretty powerful with the courts. Could you possibly get something moving on this?"

"I'm not powerful with the courts. I help the police with some things and have some influence with them. The courts and fiscalía are nothing more than bureaucracies that are so entrenched it's beyond belief, to most people. The police are frustrated all the time when they get a solid case and the judges refuse to hear them.

"We don't ask more than that they act the way they're sworn to act. The government has to crack down very hard on the corruption, all over the country, not just in the capital. It's hurting investment, bad, and can kill it, if it isn't brought under control. I tell anyone who wants to buy land here not to. It's too risky."

"But there has to be something someone can do!" Luke exploded. "Christ Almighty! How can any government not do ... this isn't believable!"

"There has to be some way to use their own methods against them," Charles said. "I intend to find it!"

"Be careful!" Clint warned. "If you get too close, you'll have an accident, or something."

"That's like the mobs!" Luke snarled.

"Exactly like the mobs!"

They looked at each other. Clint suggested, "Maybe we can use their methods against them. It'll be outside of the courts. We can find a lever, shall we say. Something to put pressure in the right places."

"We can try!" Charles agreed.

They chatted about the problem for another half hour. Clint said he would see if he could find something with any real meaning about the ones involved with this.

"Maybe expose them for other things? For things that will embarrass them?" Sam said.

"Nothing will embarrass them. They're cheap crooks with no hint of morals or ethics, and everyone knows it, now. They don't deserve respect and they don't get any. It'll have to be something that'll get them thrown in their own pen, or worse. We have to make it where we're the lesser of the ways to get to hell fast."

They broke it up and Clint went back to Mario's for the night.

In the morning, Clint got a call from Benny. He wanted to tell Clint that Koko came to him with a great deal! He could get a property worth more than two million dollars for less than one! It was right on a famous beach with a view that was worth more than twice the original price!

"I told him I don't have millions to invest. I'm not quite *that* rich!

"He said that was the beauty of it. I could get this for a

mere seven hundred sixty five thousand, because the owners were in deep trouble and had to have that amount very fast."

"The property's worth five hundred thousand and the people selling it don't own it," Clint said.

"I figured. I said I would do a title search and make them an offer. He said they had all the papers already prepared. They have the title and the registration and everything. The new plano. Everything. They had it done because they have to have the money fast."

"Whose name is on the title – which there ain't none of along that beach?"

Benny laughed. "Somebody named Lanchester. They're in the states, at the moment, but Koko knows the agent handling it. There was a power of attorney for someone named Eriberto Cano Velasquez Rios. to act for the Lanchesters."

"Tell you what! String them! Tell them you're going to have a man there who has your power of attorney. Convince that man, me, that's it's legit and it's a done deal!

"I'll be disguised. I have a cousin here who lets me use his ID. He looks enough like me that the pictures on those things can't say it isn't me, and I'll use some things that will make me look a bit different. Maybe we can tie their tails in a knot over this one!"

"It might be fun! I'll go along with it. What's your cousin' name?"

"Hanrady."

They agreed to try that. It would be entertainment, at worst.

Clint went back to Mario's and was about to leave, saying he was going back to Bocas, when he got a call from a local police officer, Capitan Alfonso Verano.

"Mr. Faraday, I have a recommendation for you from two police officials, Sergio Sanchez, in Bocas, and Tonio Valdez, in Chiriqui? You aid them in solving crimes, and I know you are in this area. I have read accounts of the things you have done to help.

"I have a case you may find interesting. A particularly heinous murder."

"Yes?"

"A man, Koko Perez, whom you may have heard of, was found this morning, murdered. He was not killed rapidly. It is a gory mess!"

"I'll come over. I'll have to leave for a day or two, later, but will be back soon."

He went to the address out of town, where the body was found. It was a very isolated sort of place. The nearest neighbor was at least three kilometers away. The room had a lot of sound-suppressing foam on all the walls. If anything Fonso said was true, it was that it was a gory mess.

Clint studied the scene, carefully. Fonso had been right that he didn't die rapidly. There was blood all over the room. He had been cut in a lot of places that would prove extremely painful, if mostly from psychological pain. He had been stripped and tied spreadeagled to a sort of "X" frame. There was a little cloth sack tied to his genitals. Fonso said no one had touched anything here, except the medical examiner, who had walked in, took one look, and announced that the subject was dead as of that moment, seven thirty three. There was a knife hasp sticking out of the chest over the heart.

"See anything, other than the obvious?" Fonso asked.

"What you see is what you have, so far as I can tell. Maybe there's something in the sack?"

Fonso called the CSI woman, Naomi, who had her

assistant carefully video-record her as she removed the sack. She opened it for the camera to show a memory stick inside. She used a fingerprint kit to show that it had no prints on it.

"This is a four gigabyte DataTraveler memory stick that I am placing into the hands of Officer Verano for further investigation."

Fonso and Clint took the stick, checked over the scene carefully, then went back to the station. They put the stick into a USB port and the legend came up to play with Windows Media Player as the highlighted order panel. Fonso shrugged and clicked on it.

There was no video on it. It was a strongly scrambled voice that announced, "I am prepared at this time to question Sr. Serakoko Perez concerning his involvement with several dishonest transactions. Sr. Perez has refused any cooperation, thus I am forced to use methods which I find odious and repulsive, but which he will find are methods used by him and his associates with little thought.

"I do this because the things these people have done have cost too many people the things they worked and saved for for many years. These people have no compassion nor consideration, for anyone, under any circumstances. I would much prefer to have the things I will now be forced to use to continue for as many years to Sr. Perez, but we have many things in life that are not as we would prefer.

"One of my friends worked for more than forty years, meticulously saving what he could, when he could, so that he may retire in later life to a way that is not stressful nor uncomfortable. All he asked was peace.

"These people, apparently through a scheme invented by Sr. Perez, have lost all of that and even have lost into other debts they must pay. The mental anguish and pain they have suffered at the hands of this slimy piece of *shit!* ... sorry. I must not sink to that low a level, here, to retain credibility.

"I will extract – that is the word these people use – information from this person.

"The mouth of Sr. Perez is covered, at this moment, with duct tape. I will remove that tape and will ask Sr. Perez questions he will answer, without evasion. Should he, in any way, fail to comply with this single simple request, he will very deeply regret it."

There were small background noises, all along. They could hear the ungentle ripping off of the duct tape. Perez cried out and started to yell about his treatment. (This was the second voice. They could safely assume it was Perez.)

"You will shut up and will speak when you are told to speak. You will answer all my questions with complete honesty. Should you fail to do exactly as requested, you will find yourself in intense pain.

"What is your name?"

P: "You can't do this to ... eeeeeeeeee!"

V: "I have been taught methods that induce great pain. What is your name?"

P: "Koko! Serakoko Perez Veras!"

V: "Do you understand why you are here?"

P: "I ... you can't do this to me ... eeeee! ... because of the land deal! They tricked me into it! I lost more than you!"

V: "Truth, Sr. Perez. Truth. Had it been one thing, you could make such an untrue statement. I am here because of a number of such land deals in which you were involved.

"Who is your accomplice in this?"

P: "They'll kill me!"

V: "And I will, if you don't answer. Honestly."

P: "Eriberto Velasquez and his brother, the judge, Fernando Castillo V. For Velasquez."

V: "And who else is involved? In what way?"

P: "Else? Only ... eeeee! ... Please! Please! No more! I can't ... you don't understand!"

V: "I do understand. You are in a position to get some revenge on those people."

P: "Revenge? What...?"

V: "You stole millions of dollars in properties from old people who had nothing else and they gave you hundreds for it. Only you were at direct risk. If you don't see that, you are as stupid as I think you are.

"Who?

"Sr. Perez is shaking his head 'No.' Stupid!"

P: "Eeeee! Oh my god! No! *No! Eeeeeeeee!*" and gasping sobbing.

V: "I am afraid that anymore of this will leave you unable to have the relations with the ladies you seem to always seek."

P: Sobbing.

V: "Who, Sr. Perez?"

P: "I'm bleeding to death!"

V: "Yes. Who, Sr. Perez?"

P: "You damned fucking maniac! I don't care ... eeee! ... you damned fucking ... eeeee!"

V: "You see the pain you cause others. You can end the pain, simply. Tell me the truth."

P: "No! Don't! Nilia Perines, the notaria! That's all! I swear! We have an agreement and I bring the mark and they do it all! I only set it up! Nilia tells one of the girls in the office to stamp it! I don't do anything but set it up!"

V: "Thank you, Sr. Perez. The pain will end now."

P: "Gnnnngh!"

"Well, that last noise was the knife to the heart," Clint said. "The pain ended."

"Or started. I think perhaps Sr. Perez, as his soul, is now burning in Hell and always will be."

"We can hope," Clint said.

They didn't find much more. Clint knew that whoever made that recording had a laptop and a special noise interference insertion device. He didn't mention that to Fonso.

He said it was time he left, but that he'd return, soon. He would suggest police protection for the Velasquez brothers and the notaria, but they sure as hell didn't deserve it.

He thought for a minute, then told Fonso it would be better if no one knew he had gone anywhere. He used a route he'd found to get out of town.

The somewhat distinguished man who looked like he could be related to Clint Faraday stepped off the bus, adjusted his glasses, shifted the heavy briefcase to his other hand to pick up the maleta, said his thanks to the door boy, and headed for the hotel, just two blocks away.

Mario and Jessy were passing. The man greeted them and asked if they'd seen a gringo who looked a lot like him around town, and did they know where he was staying, if so.

"Do you mean Clint Faraday?" Jessy asked.

"Yes. He is my cousin. I am James Hanrady. I am told I greatly resemble Clinton. I have not met him, except through rare e-mails and a few telephone conversations."

"You do look a lot like him, but he's taller and doesn't have the mustache. His hair's a little different color and longer. He has blue eyes, while yours are more hazel, I think they call it," Mario said. He had noted the wig, a very expensive one, that covered Clint's ample hair.

"Yes. I don't wish the mustache, but there is a scar that makes me more comfortable with it." Mario could see a slight scar along the upper part of the mustache. "So you have seen Clinton?"

"Yes. Clint's staying at our place. He's bound to meet you, this time! He's working with the police on a murder!" Jessy said.

Clint laughed. "If there's a murder, Clinton will be there! I call him a murder magnet!

"If you see him before I do, please tell him I am here and would like to meet him."

They promised to do that and "James Hanrady" checked

into the hotel. He found a place he could rent a car, so did. He moved around town a little, managing to run into Benny, who kept looking at him, so he finally said, "Yeah. It's me. You can now inform me that Koko's dead – where your girlfriend can hear. You can manage to find her and I'll happen to pass by, looking for you. You can suggest there isn't any point to me being here to check out the land deal."

"And they'll get in touch with one of us in five minutes to say the deal is still set up!"

"D'ju godt it!"

"I'm meeting her in fifteen minutes or so in front of the banco. BNP."

"I'll just happen, coincidence of coincidences! to be going to the Banco Nacional in, say, fifteen minutes!"

Benny giggled and waved. Clint went toward the center to have a cup of coffee at a pleasant little kiosko. Benny and girlfriend came by and he called to him. "Mr. Goode! I am here! I was looking for you!"

"Oh! Hi, James! I tried to call, but your phone was off."

"It was?" Clint took out a very expensive cell phone and slapped his head. "I turned it off for the flight to Chitre and forgot to turn it on again!" He turned it on and got an immediate notice that there were four missed calls and two new text messages and two new voice messages. He looked at the calling numbers and put the phone back in his pocket.

"James, I'm afraid the man who was selling the land was murdered last night! There's no reason for you to be here, now, I guess."

"So! That Indio woman said my cousin was involved in a murder. That must be the one. I call Clinton a murder magnet.

"If the person murdered was an agent for others, there might well still be reason for me to be here, you know."

"That's true! I didn't ... he said he was ... I just wouldn't know who they are or how to contact them. Sorry, James."

"Do you mean Koko?" Toria asked. "I think I know who he works for. A couple of them. I can find out."

"Would you? I'd appreciate it," Benny replied. She said, "Mucho gusto!" and walked away.

"Well, it's less than your five minutes," Clint said, with a smirk. "You really shouldn't let some floozy you're humping know anything about your business dealings, Mr. Goode."

"Why, James, I'm purely amazed she would know who was setting me up! I'm shocked, I tell you, *shocked*!"

Clint gave him the finger. He giggled.

His phone buzzed. He grinned and said, "She knew a couple of them and went right to the right one in less than two minutes. I'm *shocked*, I tell you!" and answered the call. He said he would be there at four. He would bring his investigator with him.

"Well, I guess I could. I didn't have a lot sent ... I don't get it until Monday. I would be glad to leave a deposit, but I don't have it right now."

Clint waved, pointed to himself and mouthed, "One thousand."

"Er, wait a minute! James can issue a check for up to ... James, how much can I take from petty cash?"

"I can take one thousand dollars per day, Mr. Goode."

"I could leave a thousand deposit, if James says the papers look okay to him. He could investigate Monday while I'm in Chitre for the rest. It's Saturday, so that's only a day and a half away."

"Okay. I'll do that. See you at four."

"Which one was that?" Clint asked.

"Some clown named Eriberto Velasquez. He sounded cultured, but it's pretty obvious he's not."

"He's not?"

"His agent was murdered a few hours ago and the deal goes on as if nothing has changed? He's not going to ask for a minute of silence in the memory of his old partner?"

"Shockingly crass! I'm uncertain whether we should be entering into negotiations with any such ... common trash, Mr. Goode!"

"But this is a deal that's too good to pass up!"

"Yes. Well, I think now I'll go pan for gold in that little stream just out of town. The mine I'm going to invest in is only a little ways farther upstream, so there should be some there, wouldn't you say?"

"I think it's a bit oddish someone didn't find that mine years ago, but those things, so I'm led to believe, happen."

"Okay. Basta! We can meet here at a quarter to four?"

"Okay by me!"

Clint called Fonso and asked that he tell anyone who asks that he was with him for the day, going over what evidence they could collect.

"Particularly a certain judge or his brother?"

"Very definitely. And anyone else. A question may be asked by another than the one who wants the answer."

"It could be a casual mention, in other words. They are capable of being subtle."

"If it's absolutely necessary."

Clint went to the hotel. A man was in the lobby he'd seen before. He was on the bus to Chitre. Larry Simms.

Clint remembered that Charles had a detective there. It would fit.

He called Tyna and chatted with her and Nito for almost

an hour. He hung around the hotel until time to go see Velasquez. They discussed certain possibilities on the way. The main thing was to produce something that would mean they needed a crooked notary.

"Why, for the sake of mercy! I'm not about to give anyone a thousand dollars of your money without a specific, notarized receipt!" Clint said, haughtily. "The very idea! That is *not* how these things are handled! Aren't you glad you have such a careful investigator?"

"Well, you come highly recommended by my maid's husband's cousin's boyfriend, who once worked for a company that ... I think I lost myself there. You get the idea."

"Yeah. That's how it works here, a lot of the time."

They went into the too-plush office, where a secretary announced them. They sat for about ten minutes when a distinguished-looking (if a little phony) man came out of the office, shook the hand of a somewhat heavier man, nodded and quickly left. The secretary introduced Berto Velasquez.

"Sorry to have kept you waiting, but that was a man who checks all business to be certain it's proper, if you know what I mean. You have to be careful.

"He's a judge, believe it or not! Sr. Castillo.

"Come on in and I'll show you what we have."

They went into the even plusher office. Berto told the secretary to bring them coffee, if they liked? They both nodded.

It was, as Clint could already be sure it was, the Lanchester property. "The owners are in sudden dire straits for money. Some kind of investment failed and they are forced to liquidate any assets they hold. That land is most of it. I have the pictures and plano, but they do not do justice to the reality. It is as beautiful a place as there is anywhere. The actual value of the place is nearly two million dollars, but today's depressed market means they can't wait for stabilization. They will accept your offer of five hundred ten thousand dollars.

"The reason this must be handled very quickly, from my personal perspective, is that word will get out that it can be purchased so cheaply and a bidding war will start. I do not hold an exclusive sales contract, so would much too likely end up getting no commission at all."

"Yes, yes," Clint replied. "We will have to look at the property, of course. Mr. Goode has stated to me that he would emplace with you a deposit of one thousand dollars to ensure the property will be available for the stated price when he has the funds transferred. I can do all that on Monday. There is already a transfer arranged. I will merely add this amount, should the property, indeed, be to Mr. Goode's acceptance.

"You need not remind us that the deposit is not refundable, if the property is as stated by you and Mr. Goode changes his mind. This isn't about a two dollar pair of socks to match his tie.

"Now! Let me see the papers, if you will?"

He checked over the titles and descriptions and the plano, then said they looked alright, on the surface. He would go to the registro first thing Monday morning to confirm the information and they could then finalize the deal about this time, Monday, if that was agreeable to all.

"Well, I'll have the secretary make you a receipt for the deposit and we can relax a bit," Velasco suggested.

"Yes. I believe the notary's office is just across the central square, so that shouldn't take more than ten minutes," Clint replied. "You realize that is a facetious statement. I am aware that we will have to sit there for some time. That is typical here."

"Notary? Er, uh, well, that won't be a problem. I do a lot of business with her, and she'll pass us right through. I'll call now and she can say I have a fixed appointment."

He called and told someone they would be over momentarily and must rush the process, as the person needing the stamp had to return to Chitre, immediately. He winked at Clint, who smirked.

They took the receipt across the square to the empty notary's office. She called a girl in and said to notarize and file the receipt. She chatted almost formally with Velasquez until the girl came in with the receipt. Clint handed Velasquez the thousand dollars and was told the fee was five dollars for the stamp, which he paid. The receipt from the notary said Clint had spoken with her and spoke and read Spanish perfectly, though he had acted from the first as though he didn't speak very well at all, and certainly didn't read Spanish. Velasquez spoke only passable English.

They parted, and Clint said now was a good time to go out to view the new property. It really was everything Benny was told, except owned by the seller.

They got there a little before sunset. It was spectacular, much like the sunrises in Bocas. Gloria kept looking at Clint with suspicion until Benny said, "Yeah! He looks like some famous detective guy who was down here in Pedasi. They're cousins, although they've never met. It's weird that my legal consultant's cousin would come here at the same time he was in town."

"Yes. Mr. Faraday was here yesterday. He loved the view, but he lives in Bocas," Harry said. "Is it true that Koko Perez died in a traffic accident? We had a call from a mutual acquaintance who said it was something like that.

"You see, well, you know he was making the original deal to sell. He managed to find a way we could only ask the seven hundred eighty thou. The place is worth a lot more!"

"Excuse me?" Clint said. "Did you say seven hundred thousand?"

"Why, er, yes. Did he gouge you for more?" Gloria asked, with a questioning look at Harry.

"More? It was less! Substantially less!" Clint cried. "What is going on here!"

"I'd say Velasquez intends to collect half a mil from me and run off somewhere with it," Benny said. "He seemed sneaky to me.

"James, the contract was to be paid to somebody named Langston or Lansberry or something like that. This is, what did you say? Arnolds?"

"Oh, dear God!" Gloria screeched.

"I think we had better call the Policia Nacionál and Manny Matthews," Harry replied. "Mr. Goode, don't give that thief a centavo! He is a crook! We didn't authorize a sale for less than seven hundred and forty!"

"I don't understand this, at all!" Clint said, acting confused. "I checked the registro. This property is in the name of Lanchester.

"Mr. Goode! I agree! Call the police! Velasquez is a crook!"

"Let's get back to Pedasi! I want to say a thing or two to Berto Velasquez before I kick his sorry ass across the square and back again before the cops drag his slimy ass off to serve twenty years on the rock!" Benny snarled. "I've heard about these kinds of crooks! We can put an end to this one, right now!"

"Yes! We must hurry! You can drive. I am much too distraught! Why didn't I spot that crooked discrepancy in those papers? Goodbye, Mr. and Mrs Arnolds!"

They rushed out to the car. Benny was holding his laughter in until he'd spun the car around and headed back toward Pedasi, fast. Both of them were laughing almost hysterically.

"Did you get the look on that turkey's face when you said I bought it for five hundred? I think he shit his pants. I know she pissed hers up!"

"Oh, *why* didn't I spot that discrepancy! You *already* have a whole thousand *dollars* deposited with that *awful* crook!"

"Think he'll be gone?"

"No. He doesn't suspect we came out here. He thought we might go tomorrow and he'd have done something to make sure we didn't meet the owners."

"We didn't!"

They started laughing again.

They got into town just before seven. They went to the brothel's restaurant. The food was good there. Clint's cellular buzzed and he saw it was Fonso, so answered.

"Clint? Where are you? Things are getting very weird here."

"I'm at Lola's. I'm in disguise. What happened that's so weird? Did someone bring legal fraud charges against Velasquez or something?"

There was a silence. "So. It was you and not a cousin? Should I bring Velasquez over there to discuss a land fraud deal?"

"Sounds like a plan. Don't let on – to anyone – that I'm me."

"Ten minutes. He's out there, squealing like a burnt pig."

Clint told Benny what was happening. They waited for a few minutes, until Fonso marched in with Velasquez. Velasquez came right over and cried, "Mr. Goode! What is happening?! Those people staying out there aren't the owners of that property! They're just renting! I don't know what's happening!"

"That makes a bunch of us!" Benny replied. "I act in good faith, and suddenly I'm in the middle of some kind of scam or something!"

"But ... I didn't think you meant to go out there today. I thought we would go tomorrow and I could introduce them and inform them that they would have to leave! My God! They claim they bought the place from Koko! My God! He can't sell anything! He has no authorization! They gave him six hundred fifty thousand, they claim! My God!"

"They have a notarized contract with you. It says you appeared before Nilia Perines where you signed the contract and accepted the money, in person," Fonso said.

"Nilia? I never ... they claim to have a contract signed and notarized by Nilia? That can't be!"

"It's notarized by one of the girls in the office," Fonso replied.

"Do you have a copy of the contract, already?" Clint asked. "How did you manage that?"

"Mr. Arnolds brought it to me half an hour ago. He said you were out to the finca and said you bought it for about half of what they were asking for it."

"That's what they told us at the place," Benny said. "I suppose that Mercedes could get here faster than us, but they didn't pass us!"

"They take the short ... I don't know what's going on! This was something set up by Koko Perez! It has to be! I'm not a crook! You can't really suspect me of, of ... *this*!"

"You certainly aren't known for honest deals," Fonso said, sourly. "Do me the favor of not trying to pull this poor misunderstood innocent act with me."

"But ... why won't you believe me, that I'm *not* a crook!"

"If it looks like a duck and swims like a duck and waddles like a duck and smells like a duck and quacks like a duck, it's probably a duck," Benny said. Clint giggled.

"Mr. Velasquez, I will investigate this. Do not leave this town and do not conduct any business until this is cleared up," Fonso ordered, sternly. "You may go. I will speak with these gentlemen."

He bolted.

"Now we will wait until he tries to bribe me," Fonso said. "I'm off duty. I would like a beer, I think."

They chatted for awhile. Clint and Benny told Fonso about the trip to the beachfront finca. He got the giggles when they described the looks on the faces of the, they thought, "owners" of the property. Clint said he was tired and they broke it up. As they were leaving, Clint saw Larry Simms sitting to the side, behind a partition. He grinned to himself. He never seemed to look at the table, but his peripheral vision was a lot better than most.

Why was Simms still around? His investigation should have been over when Koko ended up dead.

There was more to this than a fraud deal.

He went to the hotel and to his room. A little later, an old woman in a shawl shuffled out the side door and headed toward the poorer part of town.

Clint soon arrived at Mario's and said it had been an exhausting day, but they may have made some progress. He was dead tired.

"We met your cousin. Did you know he came here to Pedasi?" Jessy asked.

"Yes. I saw him and said 'Hello,' but we'll meet tomorrow afternoon, sometime. It seems he got involved in the same case I'm working on. Benny Goode had him come here for a land deal with the same people."

He went to bed.

He was always up before dawn and ate some hojaldres and eggs with his first mug of coffee and said he was going out to the beach area to check around anyone close. He would probably be back before noon, but you never know. He went toward town.

The old lady with the shawl went into the hotel side door. Clint gave Amanda her coat and shawl back in his room. He knew her from the time he was there when the man was killed on the bus. He could trust her. She would go home, soon, carrying the take-out breakfast. Clint had gone onto his balcony with a part of his Hanrady disguise on to watch as she went down the street. Larry Simms stepped out of a doorway to say something to her. She let the shawl slip to her shoulder as she answered him and pointed to the hotel. She replaced the shawl and went on. When she was in the next block, Clint called her. She said he asked where she got the take-out. He just wanted to see if it was really her. She was tall for an old Panamanian woman, so people would be suspicious, if they weren't from the area.

Clint went downstairs about eight o'clock to announce that the hotel was so comfortable and quiet that he'd slept an hour more than usual! He felt great!

Larry Simms was sitting at a table in the hotel restaurant. Clint took one nearby and ordered huevos revueltos and orange juice. He asked what kind of melon was meant on the menu. Did he get a selection?

The waitress said it was melón, and shrugged.

"It's a kind of squash that tastes a little like cantaloupe and honeydew melon mixed," Simms said. "You're Clint Faraday?"

Clint laughed. "Another! No, I'm a cousin. I'm James Hanrady, financial consultant. Nashville, Tennessee."

"Larry Simms. I'm a private investigator. Clint is a PI. He's supposed to be good.

"The coffee here is really good! I'd heard a lot about Panamanian coffee, but this is better than most you get in the states. You have to try it. Get the Katowa."

"I'm afraid coffee makes me hyper. (Clint was known to be as much as addicted to coffee.) I get enough stimulant with the sugars in the juice.

"Clinton was saying something about some murder case

he's working on, here. I call him a murder magnet. My employer is somehow mixed up in the case. From a fraud angle, mostly. That Velasquez character isn't quite as smooth as he wants to be."

Simms tried to pump Clint during the rest of the breakfast. He got the answers Clint wanted him to have. Clint wondered more than ever what he was doing there.

After breakfast, Clint went to the police station. Judge Castillo was there, so he told the desk officer that he wanted to speak with the officer he spoke with last evening. They called him Fonzi.

"It's Fonso. He's with someone, at the moment. Please have a seat there and he will be with you momentarily." He grinned. "I mean momentarily in the Panamanian sense. It could be an hour."

Clint laughed. "I've begun to learn that!"

The officer went to tell Fonso Clint was there. Fonso said to bring him in. When he was in the office, Fonso said, "Mr. Hanrady, was it?

"This is Judge Castillo. He is here concerning the case against Eriberto Velasquez for fraud. You are a principal in that case."

"Already? I mean, he was only charged last evening! How could it already be in the court?"

"It isn't."

"Then why...?"

"It has something to do with family."

"Oh. I see."

"You are expert with money?" Castillo asked.

"I'm a consultant. I investigate investments for companies and individuals."

"You're family of Faraday?"

"Clinton? We're cousins. The first time I spoke with him

face-to-face was yesterday afternoon, when we chanced to meet at a little kiosco just past the town. He is residing with friends in that section.

"Why?"

"Er!?"

"Why would Clinton being a third cousin have meaning with anything here?"

"Oh! Just curious. Mr. Faraday is quite famous, locally."

"I see. It does seem to be contrived that we would be in Pedasi, Panamá, at the same time, and involved in the same matter. It would seem an amazing coincidence.

"These things do happen. Here we are."

Castillo laughed, and nodded. "You should see the coincidences that come up in a courtroom!"

"I would tend to imagine that too many of the coincidences mentioned in a courtroom aren't."

"Aren't?"

"Coincidences."

He looked slightly confused a moment, then brightened and grinned. "Very astute, Mr. Hanrady. Very well expressed. Very true."

He didn't seem to have anything else to say, so he soon left. Fonso smirked at Clint.

"What did he want?" Clint asked.

"I suppose he was going to try to bribe me, or something such, but your untimely appearance thwarted him.

"What next? I know you want to delay the arrest, for some reason."

"I want to know why a certain person is here and why several others are still here. I want to know what's going on.

"I can see why Koko was treated that way. I think he got off far too easy.

"Why did Velasquez come in so fast?

"I can come up with reasons for some things, but it doesn't hold up long, when other things are brought into it."

"You have been quoted in another murder case as saying it is easy to explain why he or she is here, it is not easy to explain why *they* are here."

Clint nodded. He said he was going out to the beach to check on some things and would be back later.

Now Clint and Hanrady could meet. Clint was already supposed to be investigating at the beach. He was going to drive out. Clint would take the bus.

Clint watched the beach. There were very few people out this time of day. He saw someone ahead and waited until they were just past him and called, "Sparate!" The bus stopped and the boy asked if he was sure he wanted to get out in the middle of nowhere in this heat. He said he'd seen a cousin on the beach and would get a ride with him. It was that gray car parked back about half a kilometer, so he was looking for him.

The boy would remember that. There were four gray cars along the stretch and there was a man walking on the wide beach. That had, apparently, caused him to yell to stop.

He had parked the car there very early and flagged a ride in a vegetable truck to Pocri, where he got on the bus as Clint Faraday to ride back to find his cousin on the beach. The person on the beach was just some man walking along there who was the right size.

It was more distance than he liked to get back to the car. He got to it and went slowly back toward Pocri, after the Hanrady disguise was in place. There were various people waiting for the bus, so he picked up a man about the right size and gave him a ride. He was going to Pedasi, so it would work out very well. He let the man off close to town and drove to the hotel. He went in past Larry Simms, who greeted him.

"You left early!" Simms said.

"Yes. I wanted to look for some things I've been told about."

"Did you find anything?"

"Yes. My cousin was there. We talked about old times and new times. I gave him a ride back into town. He's staying with friends.

"He did tell me something I want to investigate. It's in Chitre and in a place called Tonosi, which I've never heard of."

"I think I've heard of it. The other side of the peninsula.

"If you're going to Chitre, maybe I can catch a ride to Pocri? I'm through here."

"Sure! Twenty minutes! I want to get to Chitre before too late."

"You're going now?"

"Uh-huh."

"I'll be ready."

"The car's right outside. The gray Honda."

Clint went to his room. This was a delay, but Simms was playing a game that meant he now had to go to Pocri.

The drive took about twenty minutes. Clint dropped Simms off at a pension and went around the back road to head for Pedasi. He changed back into Clint Faraday just before the town and drove the rented car to the dealer and said his cousin said to turn it in and pay anything owed.

Clint was used to how that worked! He had pictures of everything when he rented the car. The man walked around and found a slight dent in the rear fender. He said that would cost about eighty dollars to fix. Clint showed him the picture with him in it that showed the dent.

"I work with the police here. You want a fraud charge that can't miss?"

There was no more BS. He got the deposit back and went to Mario's to say he'd met his cousin and they'd spent the afternoon together.

He went to the brothel for late dinner. Luke and Charles were there. Benny came in, after awhile. They chatted and made plans about what they would do if that judge let Velasquez off.

None of it was pleasant to contemplate.

Clint woke at his usual time and had his usual breakfast, then walked out into the still-sleeping town. The sunrise was paler than usual, but there were no clouds to cause color.

This time of the morning, there were usually no distractions. He could think through things. This one needed some thought. Nothing seemed to quite fit. It was like Fonso had quoted. He knew why he or she was there, he couldn't figure why they were all there. It was the combination that didn't make very much sense. Simms was there to investigate Koko. The job was over, but he stayed. Why? Charles had come because he'd fallen for a scam, as had Luke. The scam had been exposed. Why were they still there? Getting anything back couldn't be handled in Pedasi, if the theft was in Gualaca. He had never figured why Sam Crane was there. He seemed to always fade into the background. That may be deliberate. He would take some investigation.

It was like Clint Faraday and James Hanrady. By itself, that would be the kind of thing that sometimes happened in life. It would seem a true coincidence, if it weren't for too many other coincidences.

Koko's murder didn't make sense. It looked like the kind of thing Charles or Luke might do, but that left them with no one to testify, directly ... so that was just a setup. Koko could testify against somebody. There were people who might want to torture him to death. He had to die. Make it look like them or enough like them that evidence of the one it actually was couldn't be certain enough to convict.

That was something to think about. It would make it

pretty obvious Velasquez was the one who did it. It would be a matter of proving that he spoke very good English. What little Clint had heard from him made it sound like he didn't know much, but that could be an act. Castillo could have done it.

What had happened that made this scheme come together when Clint Faraday was in town? Was that the real coincidence that threw somebody's timing off?

A woman was opening a little café. Clint went in to have a cup of coffee. Larry Simms and Sam Crane came in, registered a bit of surprise that he was there, and came to sit at his table.

Simms had come back last night or early this morning, it would seem. So!

"It's gonna be a good day. I can feel it," Sam said.

"Yesterday was nice here. It was hot on the end of the peninsula. I was down there for the police thing."

"I met your cousin," Larry said. "He gave me a ride. He said he was coming back and that he had run across you on the beach."

"Yes. James," Clint said. "The whole family calls him James. Never Jim. Somehow, that seems right.

"He's staying at the hotel. I'll probably go over there later."

"He left last night. Didn't you know?" Larry asked.

"No. He was going to leave soon, but I thought maybe today. He said his job was over when he exposed those people for what they were."

Sam grinned. "He exposed them?"

Clint laughed. "In a way. He saw through the deal and made them use the crooked notary for a receipt."

"Crooked notary? I never know what's going on, anymore!" Sam cried, looking a hard question at Larry.

"That's one on me! A crooked notary?"

"Yes. She made the scam work for the local things. She notarized titles for land that didn't have titles and so forth. When anything happened, the judge could say it wasn't in his department. They would have to take it up with the government in Panamá City or Santiago. You'd get a bureaucratic run-around that would last years."

"Like that *Fading Paradise* book. It's supposed to be true," Sam replied, nodding.

"It's true. I know that one, intimately. A friend of mine writes it."

"I wish I'd read it before I ever invested here. I'd be in Ecuador, sitting on the balcony of my condo, watching the girls go by on the beach, right now!" Sam said.

"Not likely! It's two or three hours earlier there! A bit dark for girl watching," Larry shot back.

They chatted for a few minutes and Clint's cell buzzed. The caller ID number wasn't familiar to him. He answered, "Habla!"

"Mr. Faraday? I have to speak with you. None of this is what it seems! They're not who they say!"

"Can you come to my office at noon? They would be suspicious, if you come earlier."

"Quien habla?" Clint said.

"This is Berto Velasquez. Please! I beg of you! Do not let anyone know I have called you!"

"Okay. Hasta luego." He rang off.

"Business this early?" Larry asked.

"Not really, I don't think. People always want me to investigate their wife or husband. I don't do that kind of investigation."

"Yeah. Divorce is dirty shit," Larry said, with a sneer. "Usually some crud who stole somebody else's wife and doesn't trust her."

"I always tell that type that, if she'll cheat with you, she'll cheat on you, and if you'll cheat with her, you'll cheat on her. Take a hike! The type never gets it. It's miles over their heads."

They talked a few more minutes, then Clint went back to Mario's. It was most interesting that Simms had gone to Pocri last night and come back so fast. It would appear he wanted to be sure Hanrady was gone.

Well, surprise, surprise, Mr. Simms!

He used the internet for a couple of hours of checking on the people there. There wasn't much. They seemed to be businessmen in the states and England who didn't have any connections there.

He met and talked with Charles, then with Luke, a bit later. At noon, he was in the park, so strolled casually across to Velasquez's office and went in through the door with a sign that said the office would be closed until further notice. There was no one at the reception desk.

He went back to Velasquez's private office and knocked. There was no answer, so he tried the knob. The door opened. Velasquez was seated at the desk, leaned back in the swivel chair. There was the haft of a letter opener sticking out of his lower throat.

Why wasn't he slumped onto the desk?

Clint sighed and called Fonso. He told him what he'd found and said he was going back out to see who was hanging around out there. He would make it look like he'd gone in, no secretary and the sign, and left. Fonso could find a reason to come to the office in half an hour or so.

He said, "Adios, Sr. Velasquez!" and went back out. He looked at the sign on the door, shook his head, and went back into the park. It would be interesting to see who came there and to ask how things were and what was going on in their life.

What was Velasquez going to tell him? Who wasn't who he said? What was his connection?

It had to be something about land. And scams. He had gotten in too deep with someone. It had to do with land.

Charles' land was Gualaca. That was a pretty long way from Pedasi. Where was Luke's land? Where was Sam's? How did his own two thieves figure into it?

He thought of a connection. Tenuous, but a connection. It was something to look at.

The police truck stopped in front of Velasquez's office and two officers went inside. A minute later the female ran out to the truck to yammer loudly into the radio mike.

He went over and asked what was the problem. She recognized him from the station and said that they came to arrest Velazquez for questioning and found him dead. He was stabbed to death.

Clint went back in with her. She and the male officer stayed in the office while Clint went back into the hallway and to the end. There was a door to an alley in back. It was self-locking, so they couldn't know if it was used, but Clint would bet it was.

He went back to the office as Fonso and the CSI team came in the front door. He told Fonso he had one problem with this. There was only one of him, even including his cousin.

"And?"

"If whoever killed him used that door in the back, they wouldn't have been watching around front when I went back out. All they would have to do was see me going in when I wasn't paying any extra attention.

"I'll bet they couldn't figure why you didn't come right

away!"

"They would have to assume you didn't come back to the office, thus you didn't discover his body. That would reasonably be why I didn't come too quickly and why I didn't come here with Juana and Enrique. Exactly as you wished."

Clint nodded. "Now we have to see who asks the wrong question. I think we've managed to throw their timing off, seriously, with this one."

It was Fonso's turn to nod.

After three quarters of an hour more, Clint went out to find a familiar looking Mercedes by the curb. Gloria and Harry were arguing with the police guard there.

"Mr. Faraday! What is happening? Why won't they let us talk with Berto? Is he being arrested? Will we get our money back?"

"Investigation. Procedure. No. No." He went on into the park with them staring at his back.

Something occurred to him, then. One thing ... there were two, and only two, probabilities.

He strolled across to the other side to read the legend on the door:

Office Hours

Lunes y Martes: 2:00PM – 5:00PM

Miercoles: Pocri

Jueves y Viernes: 2:00PM – 5:00PM

Sabado: Pocri

Not an answer there, but an open possibility.

He went around the back of the offices. The alley ran from one side street to the other. The offices on the park side had rear entrances to the alley, as did the stores and offices on the other side of the alley.

A few people were passing on the street at either end, so

someone could step into the alley without being noticed. They could come back out and watch to be certain they wouldn't be noted leaving the alley. There were cars parked on the side streets, but no one had to park close.

He went along both side streets. They were the kind of streets where no one would stay. Passing traffic. No one would be noticed.

The killer could have come by car, bus, taxi (unlikely), or walking. Or riding a bicycle. Or on horseback. Shit!

He went back to find Luke, Charles, Sam and Larry milling around on the sidewalk in front of the office. Gloria and Harry were still there. They were just waiting.

Just to be an ass, he waved to them and went in.

The team hadn't found much, there. They were working on a likely scenario. Fonso asked Clint's take on it.

"It was someone he knew and trusted, to some extent. He was leaning back in the chair, they were behind, and stabbed him suddenly. Otherwise, he would be slumped across the desk. It was done within fifteen or twenty minutes of when I got here. Probably closer to fifteen. The blood was still wet and dripping. There's air conditioning. Make that eight to ten minutes until noon. I walked in the front door at twelve on the dot and it was less than a minute until I came in here.

"I think something was taken."

"Why? It's likely, but I would appreciate your input," Fonso asked.

"There are two large manila envelopes on the desk with nothing in them. The file drawer for P through R is open. The plano rack door is open. There will be one or more missing. They'll be from P to R.

"Is the order by name of owner or place?"

Enrique went to the file and looked at some of them.

"Place."

"So. Pedasi starts with P. That's a bitch!"

"No. Pedasi is by street number," Enrique said, after looking at several files.

"Pino and Parque and Palma. That's the P here in town," Fonso suggested. "What places start with P in those files?"

Enrique spent several minutes looking at the file names. He finally said, "Pocri West: Garcia, Palma two ten: Vega, Palma three one: Vega. I know her. She's old and wants to sell and move to Las Tablas. Playa Mango: Lariez. That's all."

"But ... that place on Playa Venado ... so that one's missing!" Fonso said. "I would call that a clue?"

"I really do think so. I think the ... planos. See if the plano for that property is there," Clint suggested. "There was a 'Se Vende' sign at several places along that beach."

"But that's government land!" Juana cried.

"So! I think perhaps we have found another little piece of their scam!" Fonso said, smugly.

"No. We found a big piece of their scam. A bit more falls into place and we have another part of an explanation."

Fonso nodded. "And we now have a few more answers to seek from a few more people."

"That, we do!" Clint agreed. "I think I want to take a ride to the beach. Right away."

"To look for land for sale – and who might be selling it?" Juana asked, with a grin.

"Uh-huh."

Deal of the Century!

Clint and Fonso stopped to take the sign from the tree.

Deal of the Century!
5 KM of Pristine Beach
Distress Sale!
7790-55-55

"Well! That's the private office number of one Berto Velasquez, deceased," Fonso said.

"Uh-huh. Now we have to find how the others are involved and which one of them killed Koko and Berto."

"You don't think, just perhaps, it was a certain judge?"

"Perhaps. I tend to think ... we have to find where two people were at a quarter to twelve."

"Two! I would think ... the Arnolds?"

"Among others. We have to look at all of them, but my candidates aren't who you'd suspect.

"Well, maybe the Arnolds."

"Yes. They bought some land here and would be in a position to gain a great deal, if the area is developed."

"They're crooks. I came here because they stole the money they supposedly bought that place with from the clinic fund."

"I see. Crooks meeting other crooks to make a crooked deal. That would be their deal of the century. They could sell that five kilometers of beachfront they don't own for five million or more, easily."

"If they claimed it was deep and from the beach to up on the mountains, they could sell it for fifty million, easily. That wasn't the plan."

"What, then, was the plan?"

"To get a five or ten percent down payment or security

deposit and disappear. As soon as they tried to register it beyond the local registro, and any big developer would do that, they would be caught.

"What I figure was that they sold the place to Arnolds that went through the local registry that already had a phony title issued. They saw a way to make a fast ... so it was probably Arnolds' suggestion."

"That would seem likely. If there were no phony title, it would have to go through the reforma, and it would immediately be discovered that it was government land.

"Clint, they could file on that land and buy it for as little as a dollar a meter from the government, and get a true title in the process. They couldn't hope to make it work!"

Clint thought about it. That was probably true. There was something else going on.

"Okay. An investor would come here and find out the land was ... come here. They would have to work it so the investors didn't come here."

"No one would invest that kind of money and not even come here!"

"They would come *or a representative* would come. Maybe a company with an exclusive deal? A company based in the states, or in England, or both?"

"Then we can find the company. They will all be in it."

"Most of them. I hope not all."

"Mr. Goode."

"Yeah. I like Benny."

They took the sign and four others and headed back to Pedasi, where Enrique was arguing with Luke, Sam, Glori,a Larry, and Harry – and Castillo, in front of the office of Velasquez. They stopped for Fonso to ask what was going on. Castillo handed him a paper. He looked it over and said it was a court order. So what? The court couldn't issue an order to allow anyone onto a crime scene before the CSI team released it.

"We have investments with this office!" Gloria said, haughtily. "I demand that we have those contracts. They aren't any business of the police or anyone else!"

"A man was murdered and the things that may have led to that murder are not the business of the police?" Fonso asked. "I don't know where you got your law degree, but you must have missed a day or two at a critical time.

"Judge Castillo, you wouldn't be a judge if you missed those days. What is going on here?"

"Er, that is. I mean. It was my understanding that you had, uh, terminated the investigation of the scene, as it were.

"May I speak with you privately? I wish to clear this up."

"Yes. Perhaps you will explain why a judge would deliver a warrant in person. I find that rather ... odd.

"Clint, please come with us."

"Privately, Capitan Verano!"

"Mr. Faraday represents the offices of the Policia Nacional. There are orders from Panamá City that we are to include him in any and all investigation. The transparency laws, you understand."

"No. This is private."

Clint smirked. "Now, why would a judge bring a warrant in person, then want to speak privately with the police capitan? How is he involved in his *brother's* murder? Was he also involved in his brother's scams?

"I'm sure the corruption board will find those interesting questions."

"What is this man doing interfering with a police investigation?" Harry demanded. "He isn't licensed for more than a *private* police officer!"

"I'm not *licensed* for anything, except driving a car," Clint replied. "Capitan Verano isn't going to allow the suspects access to the victim's files."

"They want to find anything that will implicate them in the land fraud thing," Fonso said. "This is murder, so they aren't going to enter."

"Judge Castillo, it might be a good idea for you to spend the afternoon with your codigo books to find some believable excuse for you being here at this place at this time with this silly warrant.

"All of you will leave. Now! I will have you incarcerated for interfering with an investigation of murder if you are here in two minutes!"

They looked nervously around at each other. Castillo looked like he would explode. Harry looked shocked. Charles looked confused. Luke looked amused. Gloria looked scared.

Castillo turned and stomped off. The others followed. Luke called that he would talk with Clint, later. Larry shook his head and went off with that part of the group.

"Totally beyond belief," Fonso said, watching them going into the park. "I think they're all panicked into acting in as silly a manner as they can manage."

"That means they know there's something in that office that could fricassee every one of their asses!" Clint replied. "If they'd simply stayed away, we wouldn't spend a lot of time looking for it. We wouldn't know it was there.

"Now we do."

"And we'll take that office apart, nail by nail."

"Then we make a careful search, if that doesn't give us what we're after."

They did a high five and went into the office. Clint

hadn't planned to spend the rest of the day there, but, as he said, they now knew there was something in that office. Neither was the type who would stop looking for it until it was found.

"What will it be?" Fonso wondered, aloud.

"I think there's something, somewhere here, that ties them together, somehow. It begins to look like this is a lot bigger than we thought.

"Fonso, can you find how many of them were in Bocas when ... no. It would be here. They wouldn't know about it before they left ... yes, they would. It's why they came here."

"So! I'll see who was in Bocas for them to make this deal.

"Maybe we should also concentrate, maybe concentrate more, on David. Gualaca is very close to David and that is a large city, where many business people and tourists meet."

"Koko. Charles would have met him in David. That's why he bought the land in Gualaca. It's coming together, if slowly."

"There's one other little thing."

"Which is?"

"Your friend, Charles, doesn't have any legal problems with the land there. It's all titled in the Gualaca area and protected. They want to earn the reputation where these things don't happen, there."

"So. I'm kinda sorry about that. I tended to like Charles."

"Life can be like that. You take the files from M to Z. I'll take A through L."

"I want to check his desk, first."

Fonso nodded.

Clint found an appointment note in the desk that said

Velasquez was to meet with Sam and Harry at 2:00PM three days ago. That could tie those two together. Or not. It would depend on whether the meeting was about selling the property there.

That gave him an idea. He went out to the reception desk to go through the appointment tabs. They were in a locked drawer that took him all of three minutes to open. It was a good lock.

He looked through a lot of miscellaneous crap and found two books of appointments. The first was probably the office appointments. He noted an oddity where dates and times were simply listed as S2.

He compared dates and times in the second book. They were all in the first as S2.

Clint looked over the lists, and grinned. That bunch wanted in the office to get their hands on that book. They were about half of the listings there.

"N. Perinos" was included in several. That was that notary woman's name.

He had the connections, here. Now it was a matter of discovering where and when the initial meetings took place and what was going on, then.

He called Fonso and said he had found a part of it. It was probably the thing that would connect them to whatever else was in that office, though the missing Playa Venado planos and references were gone.

Fonso found a set of planos in a closet. It was a plot along Playa Venado that was 5.4 KM long and 1.13KM deep. It was sectioned with Tierra Nacional on three sides and the Mar Pacifica along the fourth. That was 6 square kilometers of government land. There were one million square meters in a kilometer. The land could be bought for title for about six million dollars. Retail value of titled land in that size was an average of $4.25 per meter. Considering the view and beauty of the area, it should be easy to sell at $5.00 per square meter. Thirty million. Give me a security deposit of 7.5%. Two and a half million.

This deposit was to be split up among seven or eight people? No way! What was really going on?

"Fonso, I want to study the national land policy. Something's not right, here!"

"A whole lot's not right, here. We can go to the station. That's a complicated law, but we should be able to learn something."

They went to the station. Clint spent more than three hours studying the complicated laws about selling national land. It seemed that the main thrust was and would be for agricultural use. The base price for any other uses was generally three dollars per square meter. Conditions, such as accessibility and usable portions could make the price drop as low as twenty eight cents per square meter in very large plots. Plots of less than five hectares for use as homesteads were generally around thirty two cents per square meter.

"I don't get it! That land isn't much use for agricultural. It would come under the expensive prices clauses." Clint protested. "It'll be twenty years or more before that land is sellable, at all!"

"Does it say the price can be lowered because of that?"

"There are ... this thing's a nightmare! Maybe. It's a matter of interpretation. I think, because it's not in use for anything at the time and there's no development for any purpose in place that the price can go down to the dollar per square meter figure.

"If I didn't know why, I'd be asking why this thing's so screwed up and confused."

"Clint, who rules on the use and so forth?"

"The circui ... yes! Dear sweet honest old Judge Castillo! By one interpretation, he can sell plots of more than one square kilometer for twenty eight cents per meter!

"Fonso, the investigation for determination ... let's see. It's a worse mess than the rest of it. Yes. If title is issued by the court, according to the findings of the time, it may not be contested at a later date if the determination factors change.

"Castillo can rule the land is worth twenty eight cents, that paid, title issued and it can't be contested, later, if he's sent up for corruption – which ain't gonna happen, anyhow, Charlie!"

"So we can make some assumptions. We know what's going on. I doubt we can stop it. I think that land should be developed in a very careful way. It is perfect for very expensive resort homes, but they should be limited to no more than one home on five hectares. The area and view and pollution would be under firm control, with that.

"I think, perhaps, I would not fight it, if it were to be done properly. Our job is to find a killer."

"Or killers. I think I wouldn't fight it, if we can keep it limited to what you suggested.

"Fonso, I think I'll take a deal I was offered! It would be a nice place for friends to vacation!"

Fonso agreed. He made a phone call.

Now! Find a killer!

Clint signed the papers and deposited the other million in the fund's account. He had made the deal with Arnolds to accept one million in cash and the house. Now he had to concentrate on finding the one he could see Fonso charging with the murder. If he was correct about what was planned, Benny Goode was no part of it. He just happened to be there.

He went to the station and to Fonso's office.

"We can put everything we have together and figure who killed Velasquez," Fonso said, after they had listed their facts. "I don't know if you would agree that the same person did not kill Velasquez and Koko."

"I never thought it was the same one. Velasquez was easy to figure. It was between two people. Only one had a real opportunity. The other has a husband who would stop her. Velasquez wasn't a threat to her."

"Oh, I suppose you're right. Harry would know murder would make it more certain that the scheme would come out."

"No. He was no threat to Gloria. He was a threat to Perinos, though. If it came apart, she had no defense for having her notary office involved on the crooked end. Something gave it away that they were about to be caught."

"She knows very damned well that her services won't be required from the minute they get a court ruling in their favor. They're just like her. They'd use the fact she was involved that way against her. I think she had figured we had set Velasquez up with Benny's deal with the receipt. He called her and said we were coming over. She was almost formal with Velasquez. I could see he was puzzled about it."

"What gave that away?"

"Benny was getting a receipt for a deposit. It was in cash and there was no escrow account set up for it. Hanrady was there and was the one who demanded a notarized receipt. Hanrady is a financial advisor. That would be a way to find if it was a scam, in minutes. She had her name on that receipt. She ended up with zero defense."

"Castillo could handle that."

"No. The suggestion was already there that Hanrady had some kind of connection with the corruption division of the policia, remember."

"So she thinks Panamá City was setting them up. I see. Velasquez was direct testimony and would sell her out in a minute to save his own hide.

"She'll make a deal. What about whoever killed Koko?"

"I don't really have a clue. I can see that ... I can see something. I wondered about it, but didn't connect. It's in that recording of Koko's death. A statement gave it away, right then, if I'd been half awake!"

"It did? What statement?"

"'I have been taught methods that induce great pain.'"

"And? I don't know what your connection is there."

"Larry Simms was talking with a man on the Pedasi bus about being with special forces in Afghanistan."

"So. He was hired for getting rid of Koko, not as an investigator of a scam."

"I think he was hired to see that the scam was solid enough that they could get away with it. Koko came up. I don't know if he took that step on his own initiative. He was investigating, and knew Koko could screw up their scheme and his use was over, anyhow. If his pay is a percentage, he did it for that, on his own. If not, he was hired to kill Koko."

"He was a trained investigator and could see immediately that your little investigation of the Arnolds would expose the scheme, when Mr. Goode came into the picture. That was the one true coincidence in this affair.

"How do we prove it? What will happen to the scheme?"

"Actually, the scheme can go on. If they'd done it legally, it would have probably worked, but it would be slow and tied up. We can let that go through, then charge Castillo. All that'll happen to him is he'll cease being a judge.

"I want to talk with them all, as soon as we tag Simms. He liked what he did too much. Maybe they'll give that consideration when they sentence him, as well as the fact it resulted in the exposure of official corruption – like there's anybody in the province who didn't know about it."

Fonso sighed, and nodded. "How do we arrange this so it's not another big mess?"

"Give me half an hour with the comp, then pick him up. I'll let you handle Sra. Perinos. That's standard breach of the public faith law. She'll lose her license is about all. You can make her testify against any other extremely corrupt pig. Unless she admits the Velasquez murder, she'll get away with it. No great loss."

He nodded again and sighed again and left Clint with the computer. After half an hour, he sent Enrique and Juana to arrest Simms. "I hope he's not into TV movies. If he tries any of his special training with them, they'll shoot him."

"Mr. Simms, we aren't just guessing. We know all about it. We're not even interested in the scam. That can come out well for everyone. We're interested in the death of Koko Perez. You killed him in an, as you stated on the recording, odious way," Fonso said. "Mr. Faraday has tied that method to you. No one else in this province for the past several months could have done it. We are well shed of him, but that doesn't give anyone the right to use such methods. They're not even legal in warfare. You, of all people, are aware of that fact."

He looked wary and a little scared.

Clint took over. "Quite a record. Most of it's what would be called exemplary. One incident just before your discharge is a blemish that obscures the positive parts.

"You were with special forces in the, as you termed it, Black Scorpion Squad. It's a division that caused quite a large stir back in, I believe, eighty one or two. It was all over the TV news. Torture and prohibited methods of interrogation. You liked it a bit too much and got involved in 'interrogating' people who you personally disliked. Two of your immediate officer/trainers were drummed out on DD. Two others were busted and served time.

"The techniques were the identical ones used on Koko."

He sat back and shrugged.

"Look! If you make it easy on us, we'll make it easier on you. You won't get much time here, but you'll be crucified, if you're deported back to the states. They still smart because of what your division caused them internationally, and it will look like what you did here was sanctioned by the money people running the country. You know how popular the conspiracy theorists are getting, now. A protest that gets on the internet with those people will get attention the powers that be don't want. Not now."

He shrugged again.

"Have it your way, Mr. Simms. Here are the formal

charges. You're entitled to a copy for your lawyer, assuming you can even get one who will handle such a lost case. You will notice that it is listed as extremely heinous. The charges, with cooperation, would be simple murder. A plea of guilty would get you minimum. This will get you maximum," Fonso said. "If Koko hadn't been such an odious person, this charge would be automatic and I would press the heinous factor."

"Clint, you're in the biz. What's my best deal?"

"All I want is to know the whole story. Did you do it on your own, or was it part of your job? That kind of thing."

"In other words, rat them out."

"No. In other words, the truth. It wouldn't do any good to rat anyone out. They don't work that way, here."

"It true you're guilty until proven innocent, here?"

"With solid evidence, which we have, yes," Fonso answered.

"So I have to prove a negative?"

"If you consider innocence negative."

He thought a minute. "I did the part with Koko on what I call my own advice. He wasn't nearly so much in as you may think. He was stupid and easy to manipulate. Pay him a hundred bucks and promise more when the place is sold, or something.

"It's what they told me, you understand.

"Anyhow, I'm here to authenticate that we investigated the deal and I didn't find anything wrong. He overheard the Arnolds idiots arguing about it. He was going to cause us trouble. He was going to try to blackmail his way into the deal.

"Faraday came to town. We half expected that. We – I say 'we' when I mean the group – would be shocked that they were crooks and would pay them out with the strict understanding they would never again get involved with anything dishonest. The group would inform the investors in the states and England that *we* had discovered the theft and had made it right, even though it cost us, personally. Right is right and all that!

"It was a psychological kind of ploy. Reverse psychology. It would be good for Panamá, in that it would start a very large investment in Pacific property development. We would make a few millions, Panamá would make a few billions. Everyone agreed about that, but the Arnolds fuckheads wanted to make it more crooked to make more money.

"What I had to know from Koko was if they were behind his blackmail. I wouldn't put it past them for a picosecond. You heard the recording. They weren't. Koko couldn't blackmail anyone again.

"What made this thing go to hell was that Goode person. When he got with Clint, I tried to warn them to lay very low until they were gone. It was damage control, with the Arnolds. That Gloria bitch kept getting in the way. I wanted to know how deep anyone else was with her.

"Anyhow, the only way left out was to expose Velasquez and his brother. They would weather a little thing like that and we could continue with it, as planned, only with a little delay.

"I couldn't think of any way to change that recording. I didn't want the notary mentioned, because that would lead to some pretty mean confrontations. She would see that she was planned to be dumped from the first. Velasquez would hold that over her head. Koko shouldn't have known about her.

"I think she or the Arnolds bitch croaked Berto. That wasn't me, and none of the others – well, Luke could probably do it, but he wouldn't – had the spine.

"I don't know what will happen to the deal, now."

"If they'll make a few strict regulatory clauses, it will go on. I agree that it could be good for Panamá," Fonso replied. "It will automatically get Castillo out of office, at the same time. That can only be good for the country."

"Is it true we could have done it all legally, then?"

"Yes. I often wonder when people will see that they are only biting themselves on the ass when they pull this stupidity," Fonso said. "Were the Arnolds the originators of the whole scheme?"

"Pretty much. Charlie was here for a group in Europe who are looking for investment. He met Gloria in Bocas, on the island, and said she had the perfect place for a fast gain. She brought him to Gualaca and he invested in some land. He decided to raise teak. A lot is planted, already.

"Nobody stole any land from him. He has a clear title. I told him it was stupid to tell Clint that story, because Clint's a detective and would know it was bullshit in ten minutes. He said he was rattled. He'd heard a lot about Clint in Bocas, and thought Gloria had made a big mistake doing anything that would bring him into it."

"She did that. Anything else, Clint?"

"What's with Sam and Luke. They don't quite fit."

"Sam is easy to manipulate and has a lot of influence with the right people in Texas. Luke, I can't figure. He's the one who keeps saying we could probably do it without using any bribes or crooked notaries. He always seems to be amused by our antics."

Clint nodded. "Just confess and go to your hotel. Fonso will arrest you, if you don't come back when he says.

"You'll be a rich man when you get out."

"I figure, if I can get ten years or less, I'll make a million dollars a year, sitting in the pen. It's worth it, to me."

"I think your sentence will be six years," Fonso said. "That's about average."

"I made out, then!"

They shook hands and Simms left. Fonso said he didn't think he'd run.

"He knows he'll stay alive in the pen. The rest will start having accidents, unless they find a way to get space between themselves and Gloria. I think he knows that. Maybe he'll warn the others. Luke can probably take care of himself," Clint replied. "Me, I'll want to go home to the wife and kids. I've had enough of this!"

"Stay in touch. I'll let you know what more happens."

Clint teased at Nito, who teased back at him. Nicole came in to join the fun. Tyna brought out some cookies she'd made.

They played a bit, then went swimming. They would stay in Bocas Town for another week, then move to their place in Cusapín. It had been four days since he had come back home from Pedasi.

After the swim, he and the family were laying around the deck, when the phone buzzed. Clint answered when he read the caller ID.

"Fonso! Que tal?"

"Hello, Clint. I just wanted to tell you the latest.

"It seems Gloria Arrends had an automobile accident, yesterday. She was driving that fancy car too fast and ran off the road on the curve just before the beach. That dumped her into the river and she apparently tried to get out and go ashore, but the current's pretty strong there and she was washed over the rapids. She suffered a skull fracture and drowned. It seems the others won't have to worry about her eliminating them from the profit-sharing plan.

"Castillo knows full well we know what was going on and that he'll end up retired, so he made a ruling that the land is worth twenty eight cents, like you predicted. They made an agreement with me present that no parcels less than five hectares would be sold and there can be but one structure on that five hectares. Luke was with me in convincing them of that. They will sell at forty five thousand dollars per hectare. That will make them all millionaires, in short order. The group in Europe will administer the deal. I have no idea how much they paid for the land to Charles and company, as you called them. I think they will have sense enough to only make a few hundred thousand on that part and take a larger profit in the future.

"Simms was sentenced just two hours ago to five years and is eligible for parole in two and a half.

"Benny went to Ecuador, I believe. Mario says to tell you hello.

"That's about the report! How are you and yours?"

"Living life in the slow lane, for a change."

"Listen, Clint. I have a few questions about this thing. I never really knew what was going on. Those people seemed to be so, I don't know, cold. I think that Charles character had a little trace of emotion. Luke seemed almost human, at times, Sam was hard to feel anything about. Like he was there the way a picture on the wall is there. Gloria was, as described by several, a bitch. Harry is like Sam and Larry mixed and Larry is an ice brick. I never related to any one of them.

"We came out very well, in the end. Panamá will get a very high class development there that will bring in a lot of money. I think money is the only thing any of that crowd cares about, in any way. I understand the greed of Castillo. He's a type. Totally corrupt and spends his life worrying about being caught, then he is and he has a lot of money and doesn't care.

"I don't know what I'm asking, even. Make them real to me."

"Luke explained a lot to me. It started out in Bocas, when Charles went there as representative of a group of investors. He met Harry, who was worried about his wife getting them thrown in prison for what she was doing to the building fund. Charles had arranged his own situation to where he got a very healthy salary and a percent. He knew how to work it so it wasn't direct embezzlement. He got to talking to Gloria, and found she had a plan. She knew a place where a scheme could be worked to screw everyone in town by selling government land to suckers. It would work, because it was in an area where no one would even check for years, plus she had a judge and a registered agent who would make it all look legal! Koko was always working with her, more than anyone else.

"Koko knew of the land in Gualaca. That was legitimate, and to get Charles' trust. It was an investment that was straight up, all the way.

"That got the US group involved. They went with Koko and Gloria to Pedasi, where it was set to go. They had miles of beaches in as beautiful a place as exists.

"Luke was the one who studied the land laws and saw what I saw. Their only problem was the cost of buying directly from the government. It was negotiable, but would still be high.

"Castillo had the plan that would let them get it for twenty eight cents. It would be a matter of getting it into his court.

"Velasquez had fleeced some gringos into buying a plot of land he didn't own and building an expensive house on it. They could use that to get it into his court. The Lanchesters were gone and that house was sitting there with an old man to watch it.

"Simple! Gloria would buy the place and find it wasn't legal! She was in the perfect position for that. She was embezzling for three years and could run there to, supposedly, hide from her employer, a famous private detective who would certainly find her, in short order.

They would find the land was government land and it would come to his court. He would rule exactly the way he did. It was land that could be bought for virtually nothing, because it had no agricultural use and there would be no development there for decades.

"The investment group came to be ready to buy. They would pay off whatever Gloria couldn't to me and would be home free. They had always planned to develop that place, from the first moment Charles saw it. There would be where they made the big bucks through normal commissions and their percentages. Gloria informed Charles the plan was in effect. She was there and I knew it. They all came to be ready.

"Then it was what we went through."

"But it didn't go the way they planned. What happened?"

"I met Benny Goode. He liked my description of Pedasi and decided to go see it. He met a whore who worked for Castillo. He could get her as much as he liked. He spotted the scam from the first. Toria is nothing, if not obvious. He's a bit of a likeable con, himself. Gloria went on a power trip, at the same time.

"Things worked out in the end the way everyone planned – except her. Larry wasn't about to let her screw it up. He could get her out of the picture very easily, and it could never be proved she hadn't had an accident."

"Larry told me he didn't kill Gloria. I believe him. I think someone else did that, but I'll let it lay."

"Harry? It would fit. He was the one who would have to live with her."

"I think so. It could have been Nilia, but I would opt for Harry."

"Lovely people. Anything else new?"

"Just living easy."

"Don't live too easy. Living easy sometimes leads to dying hard. Ask Koko and Gloria!"

C. D. Moulton's works are available on most major outlets as printed or e-books. CD writes the CD Grimes, PI, mysteries, the Det. Lt. Nick Storie mysteries, the Clint Faraday mysteries, the Flight of the Maita science fiction series, books on orchid culture and many others of many types. Mystery, adventure, intrigue, science fiction, humor, fantasy, paranormal, mild erotica, and factual.

www.ingramcontent.com/pod-product-compliance
Lightning Source LLC
Chambersburg PA
CBHW021751150726
47989CB00004B/1608